BEST TEST

PIPPA GOODHART

ANNA DOHERTY

First published in the UK in 2021
by Tiny Owl Publishing, London

For teacher resources and more information, visit
www.tinyowl.co.uk
#BestTest

A catalogue record for this book
is available from the British Library.

ISBN 978-1-910328-74-3

Printed in China

BEST TEST

PIPPA GOODHART

ANNA DOHERTY

TINY OWL

'**Oooo, look at that!**' said Bird.

'A strawberry for me to peck.'

'But I want it too!'
said Frog. 'Why should it
be just for you?'

'Because I'm the best,'
said Bird.

'You are not the
best!' said Frog.
'I am the best!

Look at this funny
face I can do!

I bet you can't
do that, can you?'

'No. But I am bigger than you,'
said Bird. 'Biggest is best.'

'What about me?' said little Shrew. 'I'm small, but I'm special too. We need a test to help us work out which of us really is the best.'

'Let's have a race,' said Rat. 'I'm good at running. I'll go fast past all the rest of you!'

'I want jumping over a log,' said Frog.

'And reaching something high,' said Bird.

'I'm good at colouring in,' said Mouse.

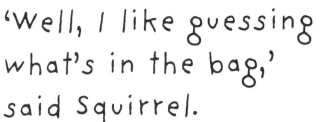

'Well, I like guessing what's in the bag,' said Squirrel.

Are you ready?

'I'll referee for the rest of you,' said Shrew. 'The one who gets to the finish first wins the test and gets the strawberry.

BEST TEST
BY SHREW

RUN!

START

JUMP!

Reach HIGH!

Col

FIRST PLACE PRIZE

FINISH

FUNNY face

GUESS what's in the bag

R!

Are you steady?
Then ...

... Go!' shouted Shrew.

Rat ran fast.

Frog hopped over the log.

Mouse slid under it.

Squirrel scrabbled over it. And Bird flew.

Bird couldn't guess what
was in the bag until
Squirrel gave her a clue.

When it came to the last test in the race,
Frog showed them all how to make a silly face.

So, they finished the
Best Test race together.

'I declare you to ALL be the best!' laughed Shrew.

'But what are you going to do about the strawberry?'

'Share it!' said Rat.

But then...

'Uh-oh! Look at that!' said Bird.

'Snail!' said Squirrel.
'That strawberry was for whoever won the Best Test Race!'

'I know,' said Snail.
'And I won it!

'How can that possibly be?' said Rat. 'Everybody knows that snails are slow.'

'Just look at my trail,' said Snail.
'I went the shortest way.'

'That's Cheating!'
said Frog.

'It's not,' said Shrew.
'Snail did what we said 'the Best' had to do.'

'So the rest of us aren't the best?' sighed Mouse.

'Yes, you are!' said Snail.
'None of you failed, because your funny
test to find 'the best' has made you all...

... best friends!'

Meet the creators

Author

Pippa Goodhart

When I was a child I didn't feel that I was 'the best' at anything. I had a big brother and a small sister, so I wasn't the biggest or the smallest in my family. I was the slowest in my class at school at learning to read. I didn't win running races. But I did have a lovely best friend called Sarah, and I was happy.

I loved drawing the illustrations for Best Test, with all of Pippa's cute and quirky characters. In the race, each animal had something they were good at, so it was fun to show them all trying out each others' talents. I tried to make the illustrations show extra moments of friendship between the characters that aren't in the text, so you can spot them as you read. This especially worked well when the characters all made funny faces — so that's why the endpapers of this book have all the animals doing as many funny faces as they can. They are being silly, playing around, and you can see they truly are all best of friends!

Illustrator

Anna Doherty